"We're detectives, aren't we?" Timothy asked Titus and Sarah-Jane. "Let's go outside to where those people were talking, and look for clues."

Sure enough, they found two sets of footprints in front of the church.

"What are those funny, little holes beside the big footprints?" asked Titus. Sarah-Jane and Timothy took a closer look. They saw what Titus meant. All along the outside edge of the right-shoe footprints, there was a trail of little, round holes.

"But what does it mean?" asked Sarah-Jane.

THE MYSTERY OF THE
GOLDEN PELICAN

Elspeth Campbell Murphy
Illustrated by Chris Wold Dyrud

Chariot Books™
David C. Cook Publishing Co.

A Wise Owl Book
Published by Chariot Books™,
an imprint of David C. Cook Publishing Co.
David C. Cook Publishing Co., Elgin, Illinois 60120
David C. Cook Publishing Co., Weston, Ontario

THE MYSTERY OF THE GOLDEN PELICAN
© 1990 by Elspeth Campbell Murphy for text and Chris Wold Dyrud
for illustrations

Cover design by Stephen D. Smith
First printing, 1990
Printed in the United States of America
94 93 92 91 90 5 4 3 2 1

Library of Congress Cataloging-in-Publication Data
Murphy, Elspeth Campbell.
   The mystery of the golden pelican / Elspeth Campbell Murphy;
illustrated by Chris Wold Dyrud.
       p. cm.—(The Beatitudes mysteries)
   "A Wise owl book"—T.p. verso.
   Summary: Three cousin detectives appreciate the Beatitude, "Blessed
are those who mourn, for they will be comforted," when they figure
out the meaning of a sick man's cryptic words about a pelican.
   ISBN 1-55513-896-9
   [1. Beatitudes—Fiction. 2. Cousins—Fiction. 3. Mystery and
detective stories.] I. Dyrud, Chris Wold, ill. II. Title.
III. Series: Murphy, Elspeth Campbell. Beatitudes mysteries.
PZ7.M95316Mybf   1990
[Fic]—dc20   89-39822
                                                                      CIP
                                                                       AC

CONTENTS

1 In the Bell Tower — 7

2 The Strange Conversation — 10

3 The Search — 13

4 Another Search — 17

5 Clues in the Snow — 21

6 Terrible and Sweet — 24

7 A Trip to the Hospital — 31

8 A Wild-Goose Chase? — 34

9 Comforted — 39

10 Happy New Year! — 43

"Blessed are those who mourn,
for they will be comforted."
Matthew 5:4 (NIV)

1
IN THE BELL TOWER

It was quiet and cold in the bell tower of the old church. The three cousins were quiet, too, each looking out in a different direction and thinking private thoughts.

Sarah-Jane was thinking that she wouldn't want to be up here at midnight. That was because today was New Year's Eve, and the church was having a watch night service.

A little before midnight, the bell would begin ringing. Slow and muffled at first, it would say good-bye to the old year. People would hear it and think seriously about all their sadnesses and all the things they were sorry for. Then, right at midnight, the bell would ring loud and wild and joyful to say hello to the new year. Hello to a new beginning.

Sarah-Jane loved New Year's Eve. She could hardly wait.

She and her two cousins, Timothy Dawson and Titus McKay, were visiting their grandparents, Pastor and Mrs. Gordon.

The cousins were on their own for a little while this afternoon, because both their grandparents had emergencies. People were always coming to Pastor and Mrs. Gordon for help with their problems. Right now their grandmother was visiting a girl in the hospital. And their grandfather was talking to someone downstairs in his study.

So Timothy, Titus, and Sarah-Jane were on their own in the quiet little church.

The cousins had figured out something important back when they were still little. And that was, that you got to do a whole lot more stuff on your own if you didn't run.

This didn't mean that they understood *why* kids not running was so important to grownups. They just knew that if you promised not to run, and kept your promise, you got to go more places.

It was a trade-off. Sure, running and yelling up and down hallways and stairways felt great. But it didn't last long. Before you knew it, you would be sitting in a row on cold, metal folding chairs—bored out of your mind—while the adults went on with their work.

Even though it was hard to make your legs obey you and just walk, Sarah-Jane and the boys figured it was worth it. It was worth it to be allowed to climb by themselves up to the bell tower—one of their all-time favorite places.

Sarah-Jane was proud that she and the boys were the kind of grandkids who didn't run around and wreck things. Still, it was cold in the bell tower, and she was wondering what they could do next.

She was so busy thinking about all this, that she almost didn't hear the voices.

It sounded like two people, a man and a lady. They were down below, outside the front door. The voices sounded upset.

The cousins glanced at one another. What was going on?

2
THE STRANGE CONVERSATION

The bell tower stuck up from the middle of the church roof. So although the cousins could see far out from there, they couldn't see straight down. The church roof got in the way.

They could hear the voices in the clear, winter air. They could tell that it was a man and a woman talking. But the cousins couldn't see what the people looked like.

"Locked!" said the man.

"I was afraid it would be," said the woman. "If we want to get in, we'll just have to come back for the service tonight."

"This is crazy," said the man. "We don't even know what Uncle Frederick was talking about. He has a fever. He's not thinking clearly."

"I know," said the woman. "It's just that Uncle Frederick seems so *distressed*. If we can only figure out what he's talking about, maybe we can put his mind at ease."

"Maybe he doesn't mean anything, Sis. He just keeps saying, 'Trinity Church . . . take pelican! Trinity Church . . . take pelican!' What kind of sense does that make?"

His sister sighed. "It doesn't make any sense at all. But this is the only Trinity Church in town, and it won't hurt to at least look around."

Her brother asked, "And what if we do find a pelican, of all things? What then? Do we take it?"

"Well, we could borrow it, I suppose. . . ."

"With or without permission? Never mind, Sis. One step at a time. We'll come back tonight and case the joint."

The lady gasped. "That's no way to talk about a church!"

The man laughed. "Sorry. This whole thing is just so crazy. 'Trinity Church . . . take pelican!' Honestly. But, come on. Visiting hours have

already started. If Uncle Frederick doesn't see us, he'll be even more upset."

The voices went off around the side of the church, and then the cousins heard a car drive away.

Sarah-Jane, Timothy, and Titus all stared at one another. As members of the Three Cousins Detective Club, they had come across a lot of mysteries. But this was definitely one of the strangest.

Sarah-Jane said what they were all thinking. "A *pelican*? In a *church*?"

12

3
THE SEARCH

Timothy said, "Those people weren't talking about a real pelican, were they? I mean, pelicans have to live by the ocean. We're not by the ocean."

Titus said, "They must have meant a decoration pelican. This church is full of decorations."

That was certainly true. Their grandparents' church was over a hundred years old. Sarah-Jane's parents, who knew a lot about old buildings, said it was a fine example of the "Victorian Gothic" style. Whatever it was, it was very fancy. Sarah-Jane loved it.

She frowned thoughtfully. She was sure she practically knew all the decorations by heart. But she had never seen a pelican.

"Where's the pelican decoration?" she asked

the boys. "And why would you have a pelican in church in the first place?"

Titus shrugged. "Beats me. But if there *is* a pelican, it sounds like those people want to find it and take it."

"We've got to watch out for that," said Timothy. "Here's the plan. Let's go find the pelican now, so we can keep an eye on it during the service tonight."

"If there even is a pelican," said Sarah-Jane.

"If there even is a pelican," agreed the boys.

They were glad to get back downstairs to the warmth of the sanctuary. They took off their coats and got to work.

They searched high and low. They saw the Bible-story pictures in the stained-glass windows. They saw carved lions and lambs and doves and fish and grape vines and, of course, crosses. But no pelicans.

But then, they hadn't really expected to find a pelican. They all flopped down on a pew to rest. It wasn't that they were tired, exactly. But they were discouraged. And that sometimes felt the same as being tired.

Sarah-Jane said, "I think the man was right. I think their Uncle Frederick was talking crazy because he had a real high fever."

Timothy and Titus agreed with her. It wasn't a very satisfying answer, but at least it made sense.

They heard the study door open and the visitor saying good-bye, so they went to check in with their grandfather.

A second visitor was coming in just as the first visitor was going out. So, even though their grandfather was glad to see them, there wasn't time to tell him everything that had happened.

There was just enough time for a quick question. It sounded so silly that Sarah-Jane felt a little embarrassed to ask it out loud. But Grandpa always said that if you honestly wanted to know something, there was no such thing as a stupid question. So she said, "Grandpa . . . would it make sense for someone to plan on stealing a *pelican* from this church?"

Grandpa looked at her in surprise. "No, Sweetheart. Our pelican was stolen years ago."

4
ANOTHER SEARCH

"Curiouser and curiouser," said Titus when they were back in the sanctuary.

"Weirder and weirder," agreed Timothy.

"I don't get it," said Sarah-Jane. "Why would this Uncle Frederick want his niece and nephew to take a pelican that was already stolen a long time ago?"

The boys shrugged. They couldn't come up with an answer for that.

Sarah-Jane couldn't come up with an answer, either. But she thought about it out loud. "Of course, we don't know for sure that the niece and nephew are even going to steal it. They sounded more like they were just thinking it over. And now, they can't even be tempted, because there's no pelican to steal."

She paused as a new thought struck her. "And there's no pelican for us to watch over, either. There goes our detective work."

But Timothy had another idea. He said, "The man and lady don't know that our pelican is long gone. And they're coming to the service tonight. So we should still keep an eye on them in case they decide to steal something else instead."

Sarah-Jane and Titus agreed that this was an excellent suggestion. Then it hit them that they had no idea what these two people looked like.

But Timothy wasn't discouraged. He tossed Sarah-Jane and Titus their coats and said, "We're detectives, aren't we? What are we waiting for? Let's go outside to where those people were talking, and look for clues."

They went to the front of the church, because that's where the voices had come from.

Sure enough, they found two sets of footprints. Large ones for the man. (They were kind of lopsided.) And small ones for the lady.

The footprints came from around the side of the church, up to the front door, and then back the way they had come.

On the other side of the church there was a door near the pastor's study that was usually unlocked. But the footprints didn't head that way. The cousins figured that the people were hoping they could get in the front door and look around without being seen. But the front door was locked, so their plan hadn't worked.

Finding the footprints gave the cousins a boost. Of course, they knew that footprints *had* to be there. But it was still nice when proof worked out the way it was supposed to.

"What are those funny, little holes beside the

big footprints?'' asked Titus.

Sarah-Jane and Timothy went over to take a closer look—being careful not to mess up the footprints any more than they had to. They saw what Titus meant. All along the outside edge of the man's right-shoe footprints, there was a trail of little, round holes.

"But what does it mean?" asked Sarah-Jane. The boys shrugged. It seemed to Sarah-Jane that they had been doing that a lot lately. She didn't worry about it too much, though, because something else caught her eye. Excitedly she picked it up.

At last. A clue that made sense.

5

CLUES IN THE SNOW

Sarah-Jane held the evidence out to Timothy and Titus. She said, "The lady we're looking for was wearing a red coat. And here's the button that proves it."

From the looks on their faces, Sarah-Jane could tell that the boys were impressed and doubtful all at the same time.

Titus asked, "How do you know it's the lady's button and not the man's?"

Sarah-Jane thought a moment. How *did* she know? Then she had it. She told the boys, "OK. Close your eyes and picture a lot of people going by on the street. It's a cold day, so they're all wearing overcoats. You might see a lot of red coats, but they're all ladies' coats. Men's over-coats are usually brown or black or gray or navy. A man could have a red jacket. But jackets usually have zippers."

"I'll buy that," said Timothy. "But how do you know that the button was from this lady's coat?"

Sarah-Jane had an answer for that, too. "Because it snowed last night," she explained. "If somebody else lost the button before it snowed, then the button would have gotten covered up. And we know that no one else came by here after it snowed, because there are only these two sets of tracks, besides ours."

To Sarah-Jane's great delight, Timothy and Titus burst into applause.

"Way to go, S-J!"

"Yeah, good thinking, S-J!"

"Now, speaking of tracks," said Titus. "Those little, round holes are still bothering me. I wonder what could have made them?"

They all took a closer look. "A pogo stick," said Titus.

Neither Sarah-Jane nor Timothy got worried that Titus was going crazy when he said that. They knew Titus was just trying out his theory.

He said that if you didn't get mad at your brain for fooling around and giving you crazy answers, it would toss in some excellent answers, too.

"A broomstick," said Timothy, joining in the game.

"A fishing pole," said Sarah-Jane.

"No!" said Titus suddenly. "A cane! We're looking for someone who makes lopsided footprints because he walks with a limp and uses a cane!"

Timothy said, "A lady with a red coat and a man with a cane. See? We *do* know what they look like—at least a little bit."

The detective-cousins were so busy planning how they would be on the lookout that night, that they didn't hear their grandfather come up behind them. So they all jumped a little when he said, "Now, then. What's all this about a pelican?"

6
TERRIBLE AND SWEET

Now that they had their grandfather all to themselves, the cousins could explain everything. It took awhile, but their grandfather listened patiently and carefully. He always did. That's why people always wanted to talk to him.

"Come with me," he replied when they had said everything they needed to say. "I have something to show you."

He led them into his study, where he got down a book from the shelf. "This is a history of Trinity Church," he explained. "We put it together when we celebrated the church's centennial."

Sarah-Jane thought she knew what that meant, but she wanted to be sure. "You mean when the church had its 100th birthday?"

"That's right," said her grandfather. "The church had its 100th birthday about twelve years ago. We had a big open house, and the whole town came. Soon after that, the golden pelican was stolen."

"Golden!" cried Timothy. "We didn't know it was golden!"

"Oh, yes, indeed," said Grandpa. "It was not very large, but it was a beautiful work of art."

He found the page he was looking for, and they gathered round to look at the picture.

The picture showed a group of smiling people. They were standing in the vestibule in front of the inside door that led to the sanctuary. Just above the people's heads, the cousins could see a little, golden plaque. It was attached to the middle of the door.

On the next page, there was a close-up of the plaque. The plaque was in the shape of a mother pelican with her wings outstretched to protect her three little babies.

Titus asked. "What are those drops on the mother's chest?"

"It's blood," said Grandpa softly. The cousins stared at him.

Grandpa explained. "There's an old story about pelicans. It says that if there is no food and the babies are in danger of starving, the mother pelican will do something drastic to save them. She will pluck her chest and feed the babies with her own blood."

"Gross," said Titus. But he said it in a serious way.

"Is that really true?" asked Timothy. "Do pelicans really do that?"

Grandpa shook his head. "No, a mother pelican feeds her babies fish out of her bill. Maybe people a long time ago misunderstood what she was doing. But even when people knew better, they still kept the old story. It's very moving to think of a mother bird loving her babies enough to give up her own life for them."

The cousins were silent, studying the picture, thinking private thoughts. Sarah-Jane was thinking that it was odd how something could be so terrible and so sweet all at the same time.

Aloud she said, "But that still doesn't explain why there would be a pelican decoration in a church."

Grandpa smiled gently. "I will tell you what a famous poet once said. And then you tell me what you think it means. He said, 'O loving Pelican! O Jesus Lord!' Now why would he call Jesus our pelican?"

The cousins looked at him in surprise. Jesus—our pelican? It was an idea that needed some serious thought. Grandpa put his arms around them and waited.

Sarah-Jane said at last, "Well, it's like—see, the mother pelican dies to save her babies, and Jesus died to save people from their sins."

"That's exactly it, Sarah-Jane," said Grandpa. "The mother pelican is a kind of picture of Jesus sacrificing Himself on the cross. She sheds her blood, just as Jesus shed His. In a way, then, Jesus is like the mother pelican, and we people are like His little babies."

Sarah-Jane looked up at the cross at the front of the church. Again, she had that strange feeling. How could something be so terrible and so sweet all at the same time?

Timothy said, "So—whenever people came into church and saw the pelican, they would think of Jesus. And about what He did for them."

"That's right," said Grandpa.

Titus said, "So—why would anybody steal the pelican? That person could just see it all the time when he's at church with everybody else."

Grandpa sadly shook his head. "Some people just want to hold onto something beautiful. They like to think that they're the only ones who have it. My guess is that someone took it for his private art collection."

Titus said, "Maybe it's not even someone who goes to this church. Maybe it's someone who saw it at the open house and then came back and stole it right off the door."

"That's always been my guess," agreed their grandfather.

Timothy said, "I thought when people steal stuff, they sell it to other crooks and get money."

"That's usually true," Grandpa replied. "And maybe that's what happened to our pelican. But it never turned up in any antique stores or art sales that we know of. In any case, we never found out who took it or where it is."

Grandpa sighed, closed the book, and put it back on the shelf.

Sarah-Jane said, "That man—Uncle Frederick, whoever he is—thought the pelican was still here at church. He must not have been here for a long time, because Trinity Church hasn't had the pelican for over twelve years. But he kept saying to his niece and nephew, 'Trinity Church

. . . take pelican! Trinity Church . . . take pelican!' Why?''

Titus began playing his word game again. "Take, take, take. Take it away."

Timothy joined in. "Take a bow."

And Sarah-Jane added, "Take that back. Take it back."

As soon as she said that, the same thought seemed to hit all four of them at the same time.

Grandpa said slowly, "When Uncle Frederick said, "Take pelican,' maybe he didn't mean, 'Take it away from the church.' Maybe he meant, 'Take it *back* to the church.' "

7

A TRIP TO THE HOSPITAL

Sarah-Jane said, "Let me get this straight. You mean Uncle Frederick took our pelican, and he's had it all these years?"

"It's possible," said her grandfather. "You kids heard the niece and nephew say that their uncle is very ill. Sometimes when a person gets sick, he also becomes anxious. He starts to think about all the things that are wrong with his life. It could be he's feeling guilty about the pelican and wants to make things right."

"This is very frustrating," declared Sarah-Jane. "We want to get our pelican back. Uncle Frederick wants to give it back. But—but how do we work it all out? How do we even find him?"

Timothy said, "We could do what we were

going to do before. At the service tonight we can be on the lookout for a lady in a red coat and a man with a cane. They shouldn't be too hard to spot. Then we can explain to them what their uncle was talking about."

It sounded like a pretty good plan. Then Titus had an awful thought. "But what if they don't come? What if they decide that their uncle was just talking crazy after all?"

Sarah-Jane said, "That's true. And besides, it's too long to wait till the service tonight! I think we should go over to the hospital right now!"

Her grandfather looked at her in surprise and said, "You sound so sure that he's in the hospital. How do you know that?"

Sarah-Jane paused. How *did* she know? Then it hit her. "Because the man said something about visiting hours."

But then she was the one who had an awful thought. "How can we find them? We can't even ask what room Uncle Frederick is in, because we don't know his last name."

Her grandfather grinned. "Never mind.

We're detectives, aren't we? We'll figure that out when we get there."

The receptionist in the hospital lobby recognized Pastor Gordon from all his times visiting people there.

Grandpa glanced at the cousins as if to say, "Well, here goes."

To the receptionist he said, "Good afternoon. I wonder if you can help me? I need to call on a patient here. But I'm afraid I don't have the last name. His first name is Frederick, and he has been visited by his niece and nephew. The lady is wearing a red coat, and the man walks with a cane."

The cousins held their breath. What would the receptionist say?

8

A WILD-GOOSE CHASE?

"Oh, you must mean Mr. Whitney!" said the receptionist. She sounded delighted at being able to help. "Room 502. You can go right up, Pastor Gordon. But—I'm afraid the children will have to wait here."

"If you let us go up, we promise not to run," said Timothy.

The receptionist smiled and shook her head. "Hospital rules. No children under twelve."

The cousins didn't even have time to be disappointed about that. Because just then the elevator doors opened, and their grandmother stepped into the lobby. Needless to say, she was very surprised to see the four of them there.

"Well, I'd better get up to room 502," said their grandfather.

"Who do we know in room 502?" asked their grandmother.

Grandpa replied with a wink at the cousins, "Why, Mr. Whitney, of course."

"Who?" Grandma looked totally puzzled.

Sarah-Jane sighed. "Oh, Grandpa, I hope this isn't a wild-goose chase."

He just laughed. "Don't worry, Sweetheart. Maybe we have to chase a wild goose to find a long-lost pelican."

Grandma said, "Why do I get the feeling that I came in on the middle of something? What have you four been up to?"

"The kids will explain everything," said Pastor Gordon as the elevator doors closed.

"Have a seat, Grandma," said Timothy.

"It's a long story," said Titus.

"Well, then," said Grandma. "The place for a long story is the snack bar."

The cousins couldn't have agreed more.

Sometime later, the door of the snack bar opened, and Grandpa came in. He came over to join them. And with him were two other people.

A lady with a red coat. And a man with a cane.

Sarah-Jane was surprised that they were so young. She decided that the cane had made her think they would be older people.

The young lady, whose name was Kim, was so nice when Sarah-Jane gave her the red button back. Then Kim said, "Pastor Gordon, let me tell you again how much it meant to Uncle Frederick that you came to see him. Andy and I had no idea about the pelican. It was all so frustrating! We knew something was bothering him a lot. But we didn't know how to set his mind at peace about it. I can't believe how you figured it all out!''

Grandpa said, "Oh, the credit for that must go to the T.C.D.C.''

"What's a 'teesy-deesy'?'' asked Andy.

"It's letters,'' Sarah-Jane explained.
"Capital T.
Capital C.
Capital D.
Capital C.
It stands for the Three Cousins Detective Club.''

The detective-cousins were bursting with two important questions.

Sarah-Jane's was, "Where's the pelican?''

Titus and Timothy's was, "Andy, how did you hurt your leg?''

The pelican had to wait while Andy explained in great detail how he had twisted his knee during an exciting basketball game. Timothy and Titus were very impressed.

Usually when the boys thought Sarah-Jane was being goofy, they looked at each other and rolled their eyes.

This time Kim and Sarah-Jane looked at each other and rolled their eyes. That felt nice for a change.

Finally, Sarah-Jane said in her most reasonable voice, "Gentlemen, can we please get back to the pelican?"

9
COMFORTED

Uncle Frederick had finally been able to make Kim and Andy and Pastor Gordon understand where the pelican was.

So Kim and Andy, Grandpa and Grandma, Timothy, Titus, and Sarah-Jane all went over to Mr. Whitney's house to get it.

The house was small and ordinary on the outside, but inside it was crammed with beautiful things.

Kim said, "Andy and I don't live here. We just came to be with our uncle when he got sick. As you can see, Uncle Frederick is quite a collector." She added anxiously, "But I don't think he stole all these things, do you?"

"No," said Grandpa. "I think he bought them fair and square. But he knew the church

would never sell the pelican. And collectors can get a little obsessive sometimes when they see something they want. They think they have to have it no matter what. I think that's how your uncle felt about the pelican.''

They found the pelican propped up on a bookshelf in the bedroom. Grandpa lifted it down and let the cousins take turns holding it.

"Neat-O," said Timothy softly.

"EX-cellent," agreed Titus.

But Sarah-Jane couldn't say anything at first. She just stroked the mother bird's head. Then she murmured, "Oh, the poor pelican. The poor, beautiful, sweet, sweet pelican." And then she just couldn't help it. She started to cry.

Kim came over and squeezed her hand. She said, "It was wrong of my uncle to take the pelican. And it was right of him to give it back. I will tell him how much it means to you. It will be a great comfort to him."

Andy said, "Pastor Gordon, what was that Bible verse you quoted to my uncle? It had the word 'comfort' in it. And it really did seem to comfort him."

"It was one of Jesus' Beatitudes," said Pastor Gordon. " 'Blessed are those who mourn, for they will be comforted.' It seems strange at first, because it means, 'Happy are the sad.' As you know, this world can be a very unhappy place, and a lot of that is our own fault. When we think about the state of the world and about our own wrongdoing, we can feel deeply sad. But it's a good sadness. Because then we can find forgiveness. And comfort. That's what happened to your uncle. He was sorry for what he had done. But now he is comforted."

Sarah-Jane suddenly had a good idea for Kim and Andy. She said, "Tell the nurses at the hospital to let your uncle stay up late tonight. Because at midnight he can hear the church bells. They start off slow and sad and quiet to say good-bye to the old year and all the stuff we're sorry for. But then, as soon as it's the new year, they get wild and happy. It's sort of like the bells are saying the Beatitude."

Andy smiled and repeated to himself, " 'Blessed are those who mourn, for they will be comforted.' "

10
HAPPY NEW YEAR!

Sarah-Jane got to hold the pelican on her lap all the way home. That's because Timothy and Titus were very nice about her feelings and let her have both their turns.

When they got home, Pastor Gordon and Mr. Jones, the custodian, attached the pelican to its rightful place on the sanctuary door.

That night everyone who came to the service was overjoyed to see the pelican and her babies.

When it got close to midnight, the whole congregation sat in silence. No one said a word. They prayed their own prayers inside their heads. And they waited.

Mr. Jones slipped out to ring the bell. Sarah-Jane held her breath. Then she heard it. Slow and sad and quiet at first. Then SUDDENLY!

Fast and loud and joyful.

"Happy New Year!" everyone said to everyone else. "Happy New Year! Happy New Year!"

In her heart, Sarah-Jane wished a special Happy New Year to Uncle Frederick.

Then everyone sat down quietly again, and Pastor Gordon said a special prayer that people had been saying every New Year's Eve for years and years and years.

" 'In the name of the Lord
The Old Year goes out the door.
This is my wish for each of you,
Peace forever and praise to God,
    our Lord.' "

The End

THE TEN COMMANDMENTS MYSTERIES

When Timothy, Titus, and Sarah-Jane, the three cousins, get together the most ordinary events turn into mysteries. So they've formed the T.C.D.C. (That's the Three Cousins Detective Club.)

And while the three cousins are solving mysteries, they're also learning about the Ten Commandments and living God's way.

You'll want to solve all ten mysteries
along with Sarah-Jane, Ti, and Tim:

The Mystery of the Laughing Cat—"You shall not steal." *Someone stole rare coins. Can the cousins find the thief?*

The Mystery of the Messed-up Wedding—"You shall not commit adultery." *Can the cousins find the missing wedding ring?*

The Mystery of the Gravestone Riddle—"You shall not murder." *Can the cousins solve a 100-year-old murder case?*

The Mystery of the Carousel Horse—"You shall not covet." *Why does the stranger want an old, wooden horse?*

The Mystery of the Vanishing Present—"Remember the Sabbath day and keep it holy." *Can the cousins figure out who has Grandpa's missing birthday gift?*

The Mystery of the Silver Dolphin—"You shall not give false testimony." *Who's telling the truth—and who's lying?*

The Mystery of the Tattletale Parrot—"You shall not misuse the name of the Lord your God." *What will the beautiful green parrot say next?*

The Mystery of the Second Map—"You shall have no other gods before me." *Can the cousins discover who dropped the strange map?*

The Mystery of the Double Trouble—"Honor your father and your mother." *How could Timothy be in two places at once?*

The Mystery of the Silent Idol—"You shall not make for yourself an idol." *If the idol could speak, what would it tell the cousins?*

Available at your local Christian bookstore.

David C. Cook Publishing Co., Elgin, IL 60120

THE KIDS FROM
APPLE STREET CHURCH

How did it happen?

Every day brings new excitement in the lives of Mary Jo, Danny, and the other kids from Apple Street Church. Whether it's finding a stolen doll in a coat sleeve, chasing important papers all over the school yard, meeting a famous astronaut, or discovering the real truth about a mysteriously broken leg, the kids write it all in their personal notebooks to God.

Usually diaries are private. But this is your chance to look over the shoulders of The Kids from Apple Street Church as they tell God about their secret thoughts, their problems, and their fun times. It's just like praying, except they are writing to God instead of talking to Him.

Don't miss any of the adventures of
The Kids from Apple Street Church!

1. Mary Jo Bennett
2. Danny Petrowski
3. Julie Chang
4. Pug McConnell
5. Becky Garcia
6. Curtis Anderson

Available at your local Christian bookstore.

Chariot Books™
David C. Cook Publishing Co.

SHOELACES AND BRUSSELS SPROUTS

One little lie, but BIG trouble!

When Alex lies to her mom about losing her shoelaces, it doesn't seem like a big deal. But how do you replace special baseball laces when you don't have any money and you're not allowed to go to the store alone? A big softball game is coming up, and Alex knows the coach won't let her pitch in shoes without laces—or in cowboy boots!

Every kid gets into the predicaments that Alex does—ones that start out small and mushroom. Readers will learn from Alex's mistakes and understand that they have the same sources of help that she turns to: A God who loves them and parents who understand.

Other books in the Alex Series . . .

- *French Fry Forgiveness*—Sometimes making friends is harder than making enemies.
- *Hot Chocolate Friendship*—Is winning first place as important to Alex as being a friend?
- *Peanut Butter and Jelly Secrets*—Obeying her parents (even in little things) beats the awful results of disobeying.

NANCY LEVENE, who shares Alex's love of softball, lives with her family in Kansas.

Chariot Books™
David C. Cook Publishing Co.